DISNEY's
READ-TO-ME
TREASURY

❧ VOLUME THREE ❧

Disney PRESS

NEW YORK

All books are illustrated by the storybook artists
at Disney Publishing Worldwide.

For more Disney Press fun, visit www.disneybooks.com

CONTENTS

❧ INTRODUCTION ❧

*Help Sulley and Mike return Boo safely to her room; bounce along with
Tigger as he searches for his long-lost family; journey through a dark and
dangerous jungle with a strange llama who is really an emperor named
Kuzco. . . . You and your child can experience all these magical
adventures and more with this treasury of beloved Disney tales.*

Dear Parents and Caregivers:

Educators will tell you that reading aloud for at least fifteen minutes a day is
one of the best gifts you can give your child. Not only will you help your child
develop language skills but you will be setting the foundation for a love of books
and a desire to read. You will also be spending time with your loved one. What
could be better than that?

The Whens and Whys of Reading Aloud

You can read aloud to your child whenever you have the time or whenever your
child hands you a book and says, "Please read to me." Bedtime and naptime
make a nice routine time for reading. But don't forget to take along a book when
you visit the pediatrician or dentist. Reading can be a comforting diversion. For
trips on a plane, bus, or train, reading can help pass the time.

Depending on the age of your child, he or she might want to sit with this
treasury and flip through the pages, talk aloud to the characters, or raise
questions about what happens on a particular page. Be around to answer or
comment. The more you and your child become involved with the story, the
more an appreciation for books, language, and storytelling will grow.

You might ask your child to choose one of his or her favorite stories.
Don't be surprised if after being introduced to a new tale, your child
asks you to read it over and over again. Revisiting stories helps young
children make connections between the stories they hear and the
pictures and words they see. They begin to be able to predict what is
going to happen next. Familiarity makes your child feel like an
expert—a positive feeling that is then attached to the whole

4

reading experience. Repetition not only helps children develop a comfort zone with books but it also reinforces important letter-and-word recognition skills.

If your child shows an interest in words, you might pause at certain places in the text and ask: Can you find the word that says *llama?* Can you find the names of the explorers who travel with Milo to Atlantis? Associating written words with storytelling is an important reading-readiness skill. But remember to let your child set the pace and tell you what he or she wants to learn or talk about.

Quick Tips

Here are some hints to help you and your little reader on your way:

• Set a reading mood. Let your little listener settle in and, perhaps by looking at the cover, start thinking about the story.

• Children have different attention spans. Note that each of the stories in this treasury is divided into sections, so you have a natural place to stop, then start again at another sitting.

• Put lots of expression into your reading—if possible, change your voice to fit each character.

• Keep your child involved. Invite him or her to turn the pages when it's time.

• At the end of each section, you might raise questions such as: What do you think will happen to Boo? Will her new monster friends help her to safety? Do you think Aladar will stay with the slower dinosaurs and guide them to the Nesting Grounds? Why do you think so? Never pry an interpretation out of your child. Let your child's interests be your guide.

• Don't rush. A slow-paced read gives your child time to explore the pictures and make his or her own mental map of what's happening in the story. Plus, it reinforces the message that you enjoy spending quiet time together.

So now it's time to find that cozy nook, to cuddle and snuggle with your child, and to share a Disney read-to-me story together. You're ready to embark on the magical road to reading!

The Editors

5

DISNEY · PIXAR
MONSTERS, INC.

RETOLD BY CATHERINE HAPKA

SCREAMS AND SCARES

A little boy lay in bed, fast asleep. Suddenly, his eyes popped open. What was that sound?

Squeak, went the closet door. But when the boy sat up, he saw that the door was shut. His room was empty. With a sigh, he settled back into bed.

Then came the most dreaded noise a child can hear at night in the dark: "ROARRRRR!"

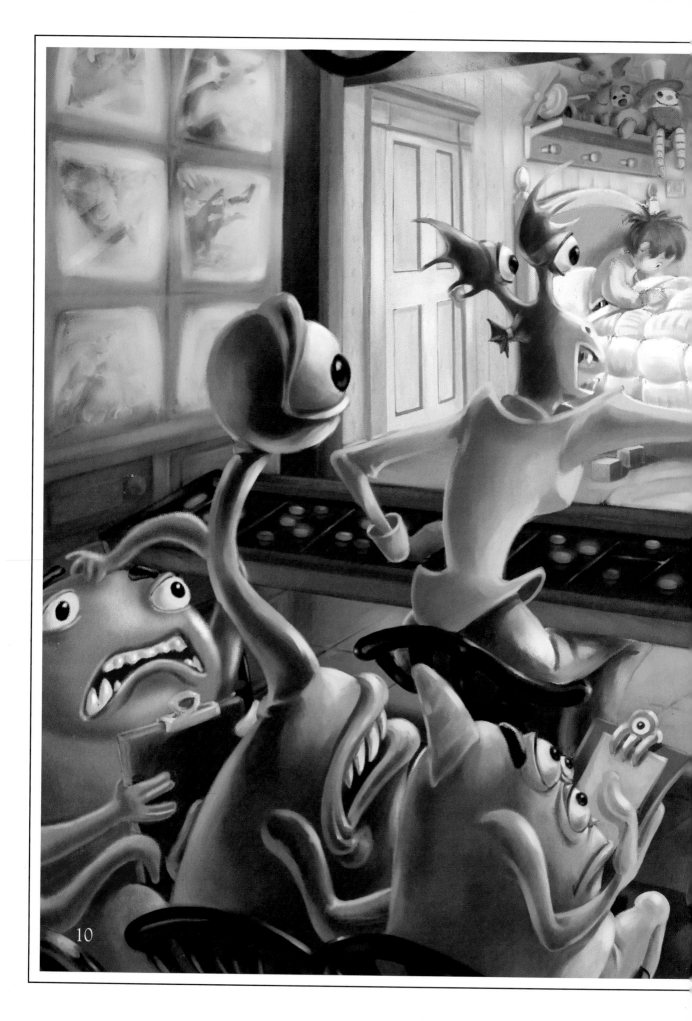

Lights flashed. The little boy and his room weren't real after all. This was a training room at Monsters, Inc.—where new employees learned to be Scarers.

Ms. Flint, the instructor, was clearly unhappy. She pointed to the closet door. "Leaving a door open is the worst mistake any employee can make, because . . . ?"

". . . it could let in a child!" Mr. Waternoose, the CEO of Monsters, Inc., finished the sentence.

Monsters thought children and even their toys and clothes were very dangerous.

Still, monsters needed kids because their screams made energy. So every night, Scarers entered the human world through kids' closet doors to collect scream energy. It was a risky job.

Waternoose sighed. These new Scarers needed a *lot* of help.

Meanwhile, top Scarer James P. Sullivan and his friend and assistant, Mike Wazowski, were on their way to work. Mike stopped in front of his car.

"Okay, Sulley, hop on in," Mike said.

"Nope," Sulley replied. "There's a scream shortage." Mike's car ran on scream fuel, and monsters were collecting fewer screams than ever before.

15

When they walked into Monsters, Inc., Mike stopped to chat with his girlfriend, Celia. It was her birthday, so he told her he was going to take her to dinner at her favorite restaurant.

"I'll see you at 5:01 and not a minute later," Mike said before heading to the locker room.

    As Mike sat by his locker getting ready for work,
a creepy monster oozed out of the shadows.
    "Wazowski!" the monster said mockingly. Mike
shrieked. It was Randall, another Scarer and Sulley's
biggest rival.
    "I'm in the zone today," Randall bragged. "Going
to be doing some serious scaring."

Mike wasn't worried about Randall beating Sulley's record. But he *was* worried about Roz getting annoyed with him. Roz was the monster in charge of paperwork, and Mike was sometimes careless about turning in his reports.

"I'm watching you, Wazowski," Roz warned sternly as Mike hurried past her.

18

When he reached the Scare Floor, Mike joined the other assistants. Then the Scarers, including Sulley, arrived and started getting ready for the day's work.

SCARE TOTALS

SULLIVAN	99,479
RANDALL	99,551
KANPT	79,012
	36,549

20

Soon the Scarers started jumping in and out of doors, collecting screams. Sulley and Mike were having a great day. Sulley even captured a big bunch of screams at a slumber party! But not everyone had such good luck.

One monster returned in shock from a child's door. He had failed to scare the child inside. That door was quickly shredded. A kid who wasn't afraid of monsters simply wouldn't provide any scream energy.

"Kids these days. They just don't get scared like they used to," Waternoose mumbled as he watched.

Suddenly, a Scarer named George emerged from a door. He had a child's sock stuck to his back!

"Twenty-three-nineteen!" his assistant screamed. Alarms sounded! Agents from the CDA—the Child Detection Agency—rushed to decontaminate George and blow up the toxic sock.

23

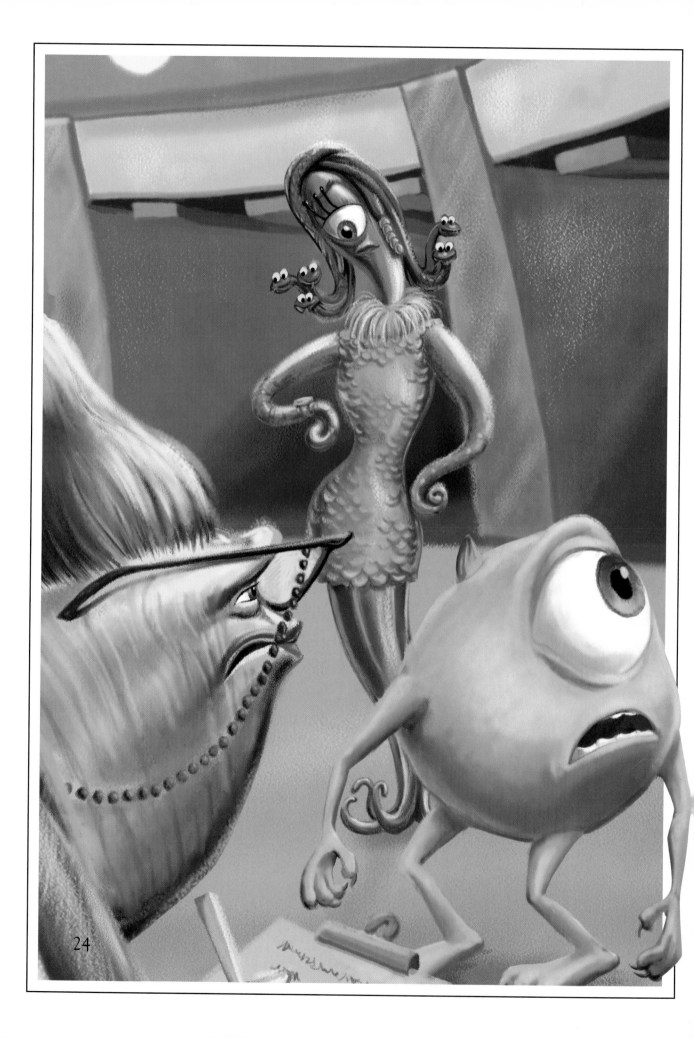

At the end of the day, Mike was getting ready to meet Celia when he realized something. "Oh, no! My scare reports—I left them on my desk!" he cried.

Sulley offered to take care of the paperwork so Mike wouldn't be late for his date.

But when Sulley walked back onto the empty Scare Floor, he noticed something odd: one kid's door hadn't been put away.

Sulley peeked warily through the door. "Hello? Is anybody scaring in here?"

BOO!

As Sulley turned to leave, he heard a THUMP. He turned around and saw . . . a little girl clinging to his tail!

"Aaaaaaaah!" he screamed in terror. The kid was touching him!

The girl giggled. "Kitty!" she said to the big, furry monster.

Sulley knew he had to do something. That kid was dangerous! He tried to put her back in her room . . . but he tripped and ended up covered with kid stuff! Sulley raced to the locker room and got rid of the girl's toys. Then he realized she was hanging on to his back!

Sulley put the girl in a gym bag and ran back to the Scare Floor. Just then, Randall showed up! Sulley hid and watched in horror as Randall sent the kid's door to the vault. Now how could Sulley put the girl back in her room?

Meanwhile, Mike and Celia were enjoying a romantic meal. "You know, I was just thinking about the first time I laid eye on you—how pretty you looked," Mike cooed.

Just then, Sulley appeared at the window!

Sulley came inside and sat down. "Hi, guys," he said, setting his bag under the table. "Look in the bag!" he whispered to Mike.

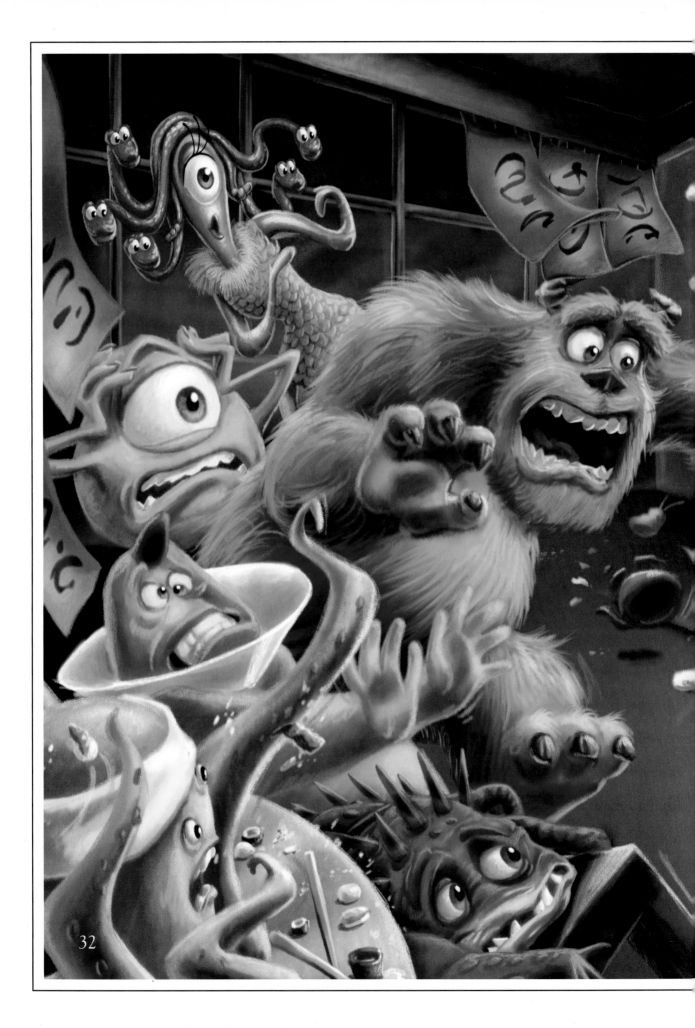

When Mike looked, the bag wasn't there.

"Aaaaah!" someone yelled from across the restaurant. "A kid! A human kid!"

"Boo!" a voice cried with a giggle.

Sulley gasped. It was the girl! He tried to grab her as everyone in the restaurant screamed and ran for the exits.

33

Within minutes, the CDA swarmed the restaurant. Mike wanted to get to Celia, but he needed to help Sulley sneak away with the girl.

Back at home, they tried to figure out what to do. They dressed in protective gear to stay safe from the girl as she happily explored the apartment. They were terrified of her! When she cried, the lights flashed. When she laughed, they flashed even brighter!

Finally, the girl got tired and climbed into Sulley's bed. But she wouldn't go to sleep. She pointed to the closet door and showed Sulley a picture she had drawn.

"Hey, that looks like Randall," Sulley said. Suddenly, he understood—Randall was the girl's assigned monster. She was scared of him! To comfort her, Sulley showed her that the closet was empty. No monsters there!

When the girl finally fell asleep, Sulley watched her for a few moments. She didn't look very dangerous at all.

The next day, Sulley and Mike disguised the girl as a monster child and returned to Monsters, Inc. They hoped to find her door and send her home before anyone found out she was there. But the company was crawling with CDA agents!

"Don't panic," Sulley whispered to Mike when Waternoose stopped them in the lobby.

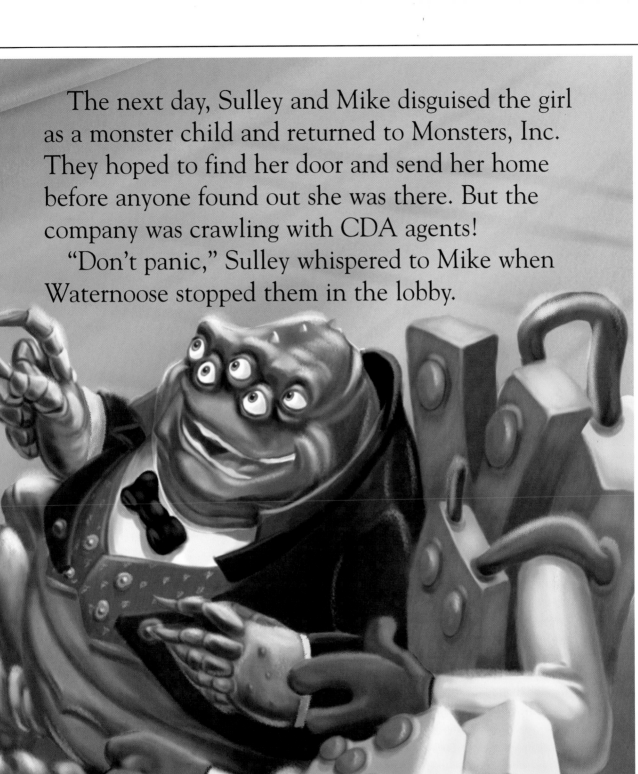

Sulley made his way to the locker room with Mike and the girl.

Then Mike raced off to find the card key for the girl's door. Sulley played with her while they waited.

"Boo!" the girl cried happily as she ran around, playing hide-and-seek.

Just as Mike returned, Randall entered the men's room. The friends hid while Randall asked his assistant, Fungus, about the girl and said something about a machine.

"What were they talking about?" Sulley wondered aloud after Randall left. But there was no time to think about it. He and Mike had to get the girl back through her door right away!

42

43

None of the other monsters noticed that anything was wrong as Mike and Sulley took the girl to the Scare Floor. But there was a problem—Mike had the wrong card key!

"Mike, this isn't Boo's door," Sulley protested. Mike was shocked that Sulley had named the girl. "Once you name it, you start getting attached to it!" he exclaimed.

While they bickered, Boo slipped away!

Sulley and Mike looked everywhere for Boo. Suddenly, Celia appeared and cornered Mike. She was very angry about their ruined dinner. Randall overheard them and grinned. He realized Mike had been at the restaurant and must know about the kid!

Once Celia had left, Randall grabbed Mike. He told him to bring Boo to the Scare Floor during lunch, when everyone else would be gone, and he would have her door.

Sulley was still looking for Boo when he spotted a piece of her costume in the trash compactor. Tearfully, Sulley picked up the cube of trash, fearing the worst. Just then he heard a familiar voice. Boo was alive! She was with a group of monster kids.

"Kitty!" Boo called when she saw Sulley. She giggled, which made the lights flicker and pop. The other monsters in the hall cried out in fright. Sulley had to get Boo back to her door!

RANDALL'S SECRET

"Come on!" cried Mike, leading Sulley and Boo to the Scare Floor.

When they got there, Mike raced right over to Boo's door.

"There it is!" Mike cried. "Just like Randall said!" But Sulley didn't trust Randall, so Mike jumped onto the bed to prove it was safe.

Sulley watched in horror as someone caught Mike in a trap. It was Randall!

Thinking he had trapped Boo, Randall raced off with the box. Now Sulley had to rescue Mike! He and Boo followed Randall through a hidden door.

There they discovered Randall's terrible secret. He had created a giant machine to capture scream energy. He wanted to use Boo and other human children to test it! Mike was already in the chair, and Randall was going to turn it on at any moment.

Sulley managed to rescue Mike from Randall. "Follow me!" Sulley cried. "I have an idea!"

Sulley went straight to Waternoose, the most trusted monster at Monsters, Inc., to get some help. Waternoose was shocked to see Boo.

"It's not our fault—it's Randall's!" Mike told Waternoose while Sulley tried to comfort a frightened Boo.

But Waternoose already knew all about Randall's evil scheme! He quickly grabbed Boo. Then, with Randall's help, he banished Sulley and Mike to a snowy wasteland in the human world by pushing them through a one-way door.

There Sulley and Mike met the Abominable Snowman. He had been banished years ago. Sulley was able to use some supplies from his cave to make a sled. Sulley offered Mike a ride, but Mike refused, blaming him for the mess they were in.

57

On his own, Sulley found his way to a human
village and burst back into the monster world through
a child's closet door. He reached Randall's machine
just in time to see Boo being strapped into it.

"Kitty!" Boo cried as soon as she saw Sulley.
Sulley smashed the machine and grabbed the
little girl.

As Sulley escaped with Boo, Mike suddenly caught
up with them. He had realized he was angry with
Sulley—but not angry enough to lose his friend.
Together they raced to the Scare Floor, with
Randall in hot pursuit. When a crowd of monsters
got in Randall's way, Sulley, Mike, and Boo jumped
onto the door conveyor system and tried to make
their way toward Boo's door.

But her door kept moving away from them. The friends simply needed more power to help them reach Boo's door. Sulley had an idea.

He asked Mike to make Boo laugh. Her laughter created enough energy to power up all the doors. Sulley and Mike took Boo and ran. Randall chased them in and out of kids' closet doors all over the world! Finally, Mike and Sulley managed to kick Randall through a door and smash it. Randall was gone for good.

But now Waternoose was after them! While Mike distracted the CDA, Sulley took Boo and ran. Waternoose chased them right through Boo's door into her room.

Sulley tried to convince Waternoose to let Boo go. But Waternoose refused. He said he'd bring a thousand kids into the monster world to end the scream shortage and save Monsters, Inc.

Little did he know he was really in the Scarers' training room! The CDA was watching, and Mike had taped every shocking word Waternoose had said.

The friends learned that the CDA had been investigating Monsters, Inc., for years! And the head of the investigation was—Roz! Roz gave Sulley some time to tuck Boo into her own bed. Sulley knew that Boo would be safe. But he also knew that her door would be shredded and he'd never see her again.

"Good-bye, Boo," he said softly as he turned to leave.

From that day on, Monsters, Inc., was a different company. As Sulley had discovered, kids' laughter was much more powerful than their screams. Instead of scaring children, the monsters made them laugh. The energy crisis was over!

Mike became one of the top Laugh Collectors, and Sulley was the company's new president. But he still missed Boo.

Then one day, Mike surprised him—he'd rebuilt Boo's door so Sulley could visit her!

"Boo?"
"Kitty!"

DISNEY's
ATLANTIS
THE LOST EMPIRE

 RETOLD BY CATHERINE HAPKA

The Search for Atlantis

Atlantis was in danger. A tidal wave was about to crush the city!

The huge crystal called the Heart of Atlantis took the queen as a sacrifice. The Crystal then formed a shield around the city. Atlantis was saved. But the city sank deep below the sea.

Thousands of years later, a scholar named Milo Thatch dreamed of finding the lost city of Atlantis. He knew that a legendary book, *The Shepherd's Journal*, could lead him to the city. But no one else believed that the book—or Atlantis—existed.

Just when Milo was losing hope, a mysterious woman named Helga came to his apartment.

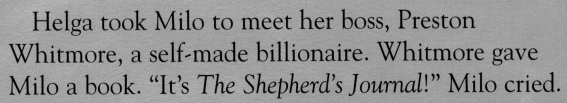

Helga took Milo to meet her boss, Preston Whitmore, a self-made billionaire. Whitmore gave Milo a book. "It's *The Shepherd's Journal!*" Milo cried.

Whitmore then asked Milo to join a team that was searching for Atlantis. Milo's job was to translate the maps and directions in *The Shepherd's Journal.*

"Atlantis is waiting," Whitmore told him. "What do you say?"

Milo was excited to meet the rest of Whitmore's team. There were Captain Rourke and his second in command, Helga; Dr. Sweet, the medical officer;

Molière, the dirt specialist; Audrey, the mechanic; Vinny, the explosives expert; Cookie, the chef; and . . .

. . . Mrs. Packard, the communications expert.
Before long, the team's submarine, the *Ulysses*,
dove underwater. The search for Atlantis was on! As
they moved deeper into the sea, Mrs. Packard heard
a strange sound. The noise grew louder and louder.

SLAM! The submarine was caught in the claws of a giant machine. It was the Leviathan, the protector of Atlantis!

"All hands abandon ship," said Mrs. Packard. The crew rushed to their escape vehicles.

After a narrow escape, the crew landed in a huge underwater air pocket. Luckily, Milo still had *The Shepherd's Journal*.

"Looks like all our chances for survival rest with you, Mr. Thatch," Rourke said. "You and that little book."

There was a lot of work to do. Milo read
The Shepherd's Journal day and night. Vinny made
a bridge. Audrey fixed the vehicles. Molière plowed
through obstacles.

88

As they worked together, Milo got to know the other explorers better. They had traveled all over the world looking for adventure and treasure.

One night, after everyone else was asleep, Milo saw some strange fireflies. When they landed, they burst into flames. Soon all the tents were on fire!

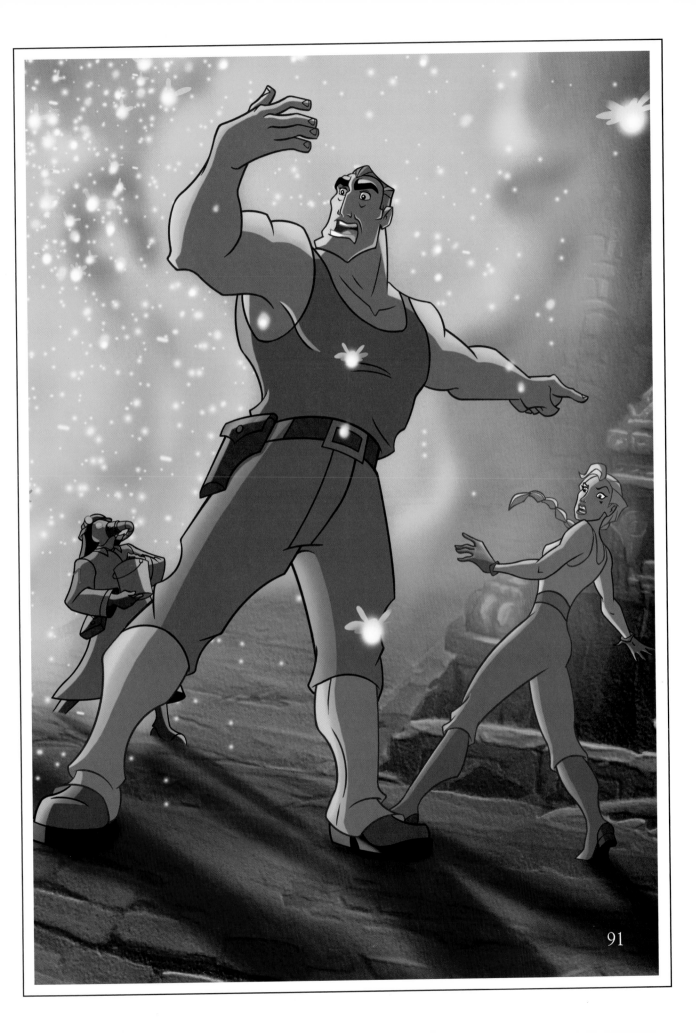

The explorers jumped into their vehicles and tried to escape over a bridge. But one of the fuel trucks caught fire and exploded. The bridge collapsed.

The vehicles slid backward—down, down, down into a dark cave.

Into the Depths

As Rourke tried to help find his team, Molière examined the dirt. "We are standing at the base of a dormant volcano!" he announced.

Rourke wanted to ask Milo how they should escape. But Milo was missing!

Milo had landed in a different part of the cave—
and he was hurt. He woke up to find a band of
warriors standing over him. One of the warriors
held a crystal against Milo's wounded shoulder.
It healed instantly!

98

Before Milo could thank the strangers, they ran off. He chased them over a crest—and gasped at the sight before him. When the other explorers caught up with him, they saw the city of Atlantis spread out in front of them.

"It's beautiful," whispered Audrey.

When Rourke and Milo left the king's chambers, Kida argued with her father. "We were once a great people. Now we live in ruins!" she said. "If these outsiders can unlock the secrets of our past, perhaps we can save our future."

But the king did not trust the strangers.

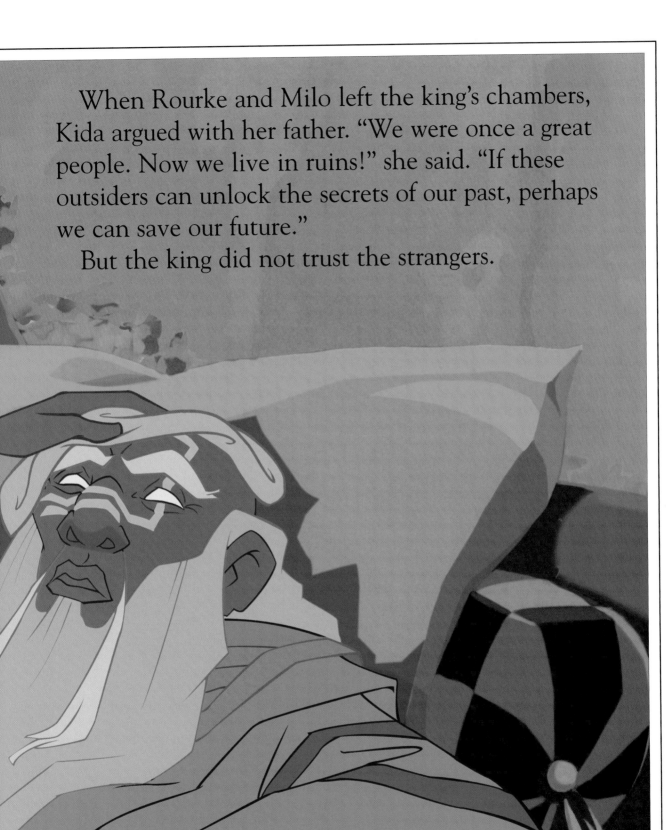

Later that evening, Milo met with Kida. He showed her *The Shepherd's Journal*.

"You can understand this?" Kida asked, staring at the pages. She was shocked. None of her people could read the Atlantean language.

Now Kida had found someone who could help her. She showed Milo a vehicle shaped like a fish. "No matter what I try, it will not respond," she said.

Milo read the words carved into the side of the fish and followed the instructions. Soon the fish was flying around the room!

Kida had more to show Milo. She wanted him to see that Atlantis had once been a great civilization. She showed him all of the city.

Then they swam to some underwater ruins where murals and writings on the walls told the history of Atlantis.

As Milo read, he learned that the city's energy came from a huge crystal—the Heart of Atlantis. Power flowed from the Mother Crystal to the smaller ones the Atlanteans wore around their necks. "It's what's keeping all of Atlantis alive!" Milo told Kida.

"Where is it now?" asked Kida.

"I don't know," Milo replied. That was when he realized that *The Shepherd's Journal* must be missing a page!

The Heart of Atlantis

When Milo and Kida emerged after their swim, Rourke was waiting for them. "You led us right to the treasure chest!" Rourke said with a sneer as he held up the missing page from *The Shepherd's Journal*.

Milo realized that Rourke planned to steal the Heart of Atlantis!

Rourke took Kida and the king prisoner. Then he began the search for the precious Crystal.

Milo refused to help. But Rourke soon found a way into the king's secret chamber. He and Helga took Milo and Kida aboard the aquavator, an underwater elevator.

117

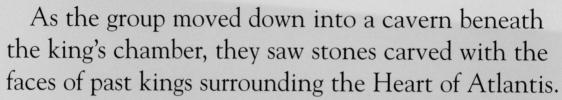

As the group moved down into a cavern beneath the king's chamber, they saw stones carved with the faces of past kings surrounding the Heart of Atlantis.

In times of trouble, the Crystal needed the energy of a royal Atlantean to protect itself and the city. Beams of light began shooting from the Crystal, searching for someone of royal birth.

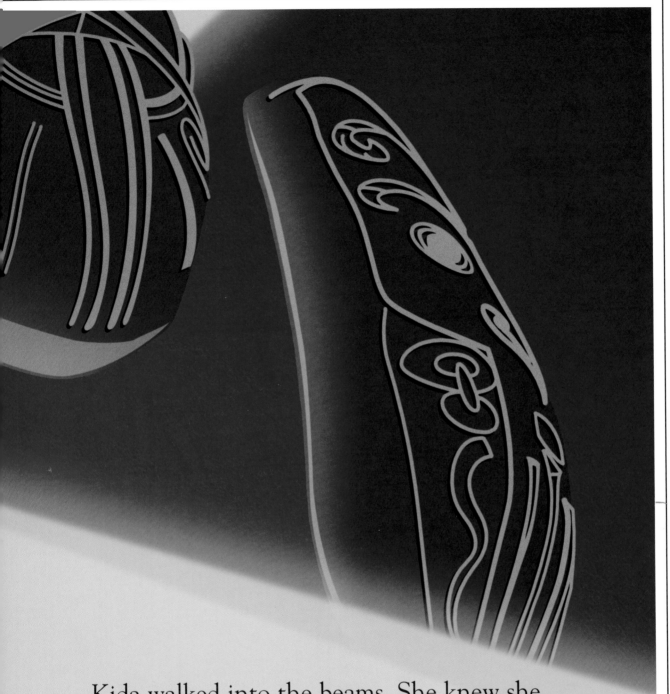

Kida walked into the beams. She knew she must risk her life to save Atlantis—just as her mother had done.

"All will be well, Milo Thatch," she said. She began to crystallize, joining with the Heart of Atlantis.

Rourke and Helga took the crystallized princess back to the explorers. They told them their plan to take Kida to the surface. Such a large, powerful crystal would be very valuable!

But Cookie, Mrs. Packard, Audrey, Vinny, and Molière refused to help. They decided to stay with Milo and try to save Atlantis.

Dr. Sweet stayed, too. He was helping the king, but it seemed to be too late. The king was dying. When Milo went to see him, the king handed Milo his crystal and spoke his final words: "Our ancestors left us much wisdom. We must build on their triumphs and learn from their mistakes."

Milo knew he had to save Kida—and Atlantis. But Rourke and Helga were already escaping in a hot-air balloon! They had found a volcano shaft that led to the surface.

Milo showed his friends how to start the fish-shaped vehicles. Soon the entire Atlantean armada took off after Rourke and his troops.

127

Rourke was desperate to get his balloon up and out of the volcano. To lighten the load, he threw Helga overboard!

In anger, she fired a flare at the balloon, setting it ablaze.

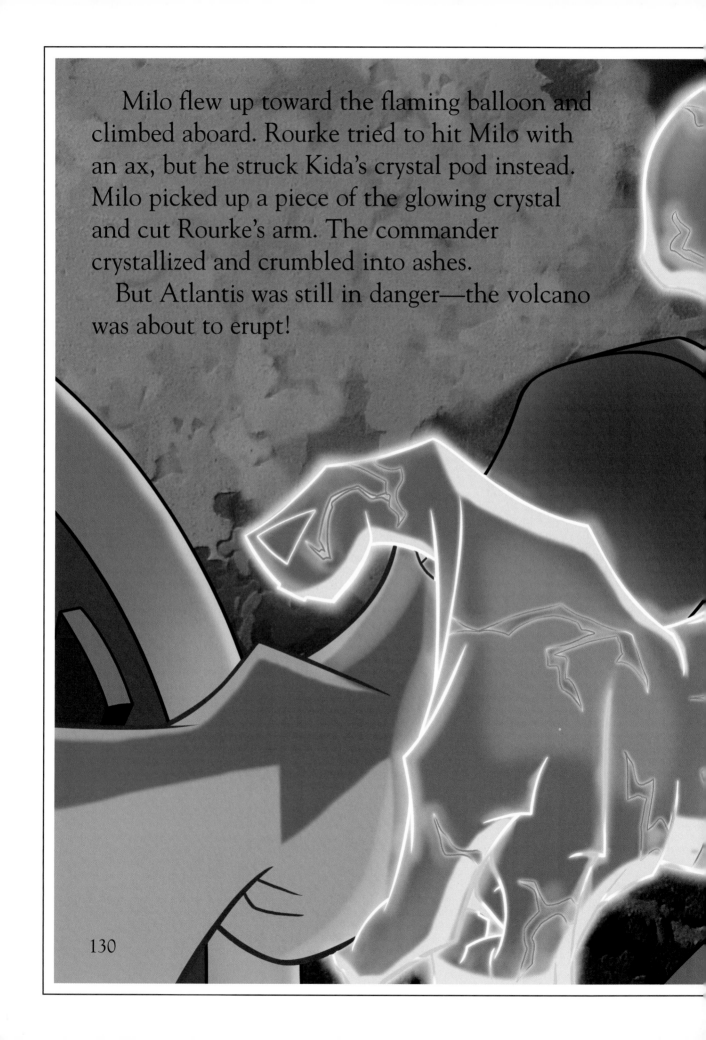

Milo flew up toward the flaming balloon and climbed aboard. Rourke tried to hit Milo with an ax, but he struck Kida's crystal pod instead. Milo picked up a piece of the glowing crystal and cut Rourke's arm. The commander crystallized and crumbled into ashes.

But Atlantis was still in danger—the volcano was about to erupt!

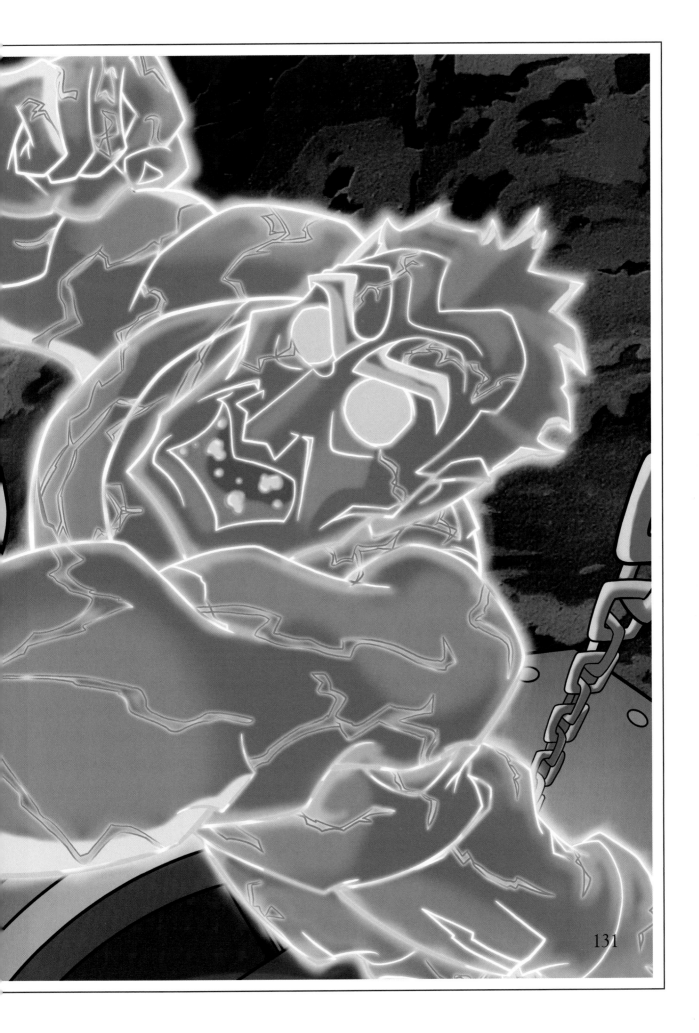

131

The crystallized princess broke free of her pod and floated above the city. The Stone Giants rose to protect her and the city as the volcano erupted. Atlantis was saved!

Finally, Kida returned to her human form. She floated down into Milo's arms. In the palm of her hand was a bracelet that her mother had taken with her when she was chosen by the Crystal.

After the adventure was over, most of the explorers returned to Mr. Whitmore's mansion. They all agreed to keep Atlantis a secret.

WALT DISNEY
PICTURES PRESENTS

THE Tigger MOVIE

 RETOLD BY ELLEN TITLEBAUM

Tigger's Big Bounce

One blustery fall morning,
Tigger happily bounced through
the Hundred-Acre Wood.

140

Soon Tigger bounced right into Winnie the Pooh. "Wanna go bouncin' with me?" asked Tigger.

"I *would* go bouncing with you," replied Pooh, "except that I have to count my honeypots to make sure I have enough for winter."

Next Tigger bounced into Piglet.

But Piglet could not bounce with Tigger either. He was busy collecting firewood. And Kanga was busy sweeping.

So Tigger bounced all by himself until he
BOUNCE-BOUNCE-BOUNCED onto a branch . . .
which pushed over a great big rock . . . which rolled
down a hill . . .

148

. . . and landed right on Eeyore's house!
Eeyore's friends rushed over to see what
they might do to help.

"Your attention, please," said Rabbit. "I have officially completed the plans." Rabbit organized an enormous rock-moving machine. But the boulder wouldn't budge.

Finally, Tigger bounced up. He could see that a big bounce would get Rabbit's rock-moving machine going.

154

But Tigger's bounce made the machine get going too quickly!

155

"You ruin everything with your bouncing!" said Rabbit.

"But that's what tiggers do best," said Tigger.

"What we're trying to say," said Piglet, "is that we can't bounce like tiggers because..."

"...we're not tiggers," finished Pooh sadly.

157

Roo followed Tigger as he walked off. Suddenly Tigger brightened. "Say—if there are other tiggers, we could all bounce morning, noon, and nighty-night, too!"

The Family Tree

Tigger and Roo went to Owl to find out how to find other tiggers. Owl explained, "To find one's family, one must find one's family tree."

"Say, thanks for the tip, Beak-Lips!" cried Tigger as he and Roo bounced off.

162

Arriving with a great big bounce, Tigger asked his friends if they had seen any members of the tigger family tree. But no one had.

"I didn't know Tigger had a family," said Piglet.
"Seemed to be looking for 'em," added Eeyore.
"We must be supposed to help them," said Pooh.
"I often remember to forget these sorts of things."

But, after a long search, Tigger and Roo returned
home without having found a single other tigger.

"If there were other tiggers, we could all bounce
the Whoop-de-Dooper Loop-de-Looper Alley-Ooper
Bounce," said Tigger sadly.

167

Wanting to be just like Tigger, Roo tried the bounce, too. *Crash!* He landed in an open closet—where he found a locket.

"It must have a picture of my tigger family inside!" cried Tigger. But the locket was empty.

Meanwhile, Eeyore announced, "I found 'em—Tigger's family." He led Pooh and Piglet to a pond full of striped, bouncy frogs. Could this be Tigger's family?

"Tigger misses you very much," said Pooh to a frog. But the frog just hopped away.

Then, in a nearby tree, Pooh found some bees—*striped* bees. Bees that looked just a little bit like Tigger.

"Oh bother!" Pooh said when the bees started to chase him and Piglet and Eeyore. "I don't think these bees are the right sorts of tiggers."

Poor Tigger was no closer to finding his family.

"Why don't you write them a letter?" suggested Roo.

"Hoo-hoo-*hoo!*" hooted Tigger happily. And he began to write.

175

Tigger mailed his letter and waited for a response. But none came. Roo grew worried about his friend.

Kanga said, "As long as we care for him, he always will be one of our family."

A Letter for Tigger

The next day, Roo gathered everyone except Tigger at Owl's house. Roo wanted Owl to write a letter to Tigger from his family.

Owl began the letter: "Dear Tigger, Just a note to say . . ."

"Dress warmly," suggested Kanga.

"Eat well," added Pooh.

"Stay safe and sound," said Piglet.

"Keep smilin'," rumbled Eeyore.

"We're always there for you," said Roo.

Owl finished the letter: "Wishing you all the best, Signed, Your Family."

181

The next morning, Tigger showed off the letter from his family. "They're comin' ta see me, TOMORROW!"

"Where does it say that?" asked Owl, surprised.

"Nowhere!" said Tigger. "'Cause with us tiggers ya gotta read betwixt the lines."

Now Roo had a new idea: the friends would pretend to be Tigger's long-lost family! They all painted on stripes and practiced their bouncing.

That evening, Tigger welcomed his family. "Let's all do what tiggers do best! That's bouncin', of course."

Roo tried to bounce the Whoop-de-Dooper Loop-de-Looper Alley-Ooper Bounce but crashed into the closet . . . again.

Roo's mask fell off. Then Tigger pulled off the others' masks as well.

Tigger was so disappointed. "There's a tigger family tree fulla my REAL family, and I'm gonna find 'em!" he said, and left.

Rabbit, Pooh, Piglet, Eeyore, and Roo
followed after Tigger. "Tigger! Tigger!"
they called into the raging snow.

191

Deep in the forest, Tigger had just found a tree so grand and gleaming that it had to be the tigger family tree!

"Hoo-hoo-hoo!" called Tigger. But no one was home. Tigger sadly dropped his letter.

193

Tigger's letter soared off into the wind, and landed right in Roo's hand. He started running toward the giant tree, with the others right behind him.

"What are you guyses doing here?" Tigger asked.

"We came all this way to look for you!" explained Rabbit.

Tigger began to argue that he was waiting for his tigger family when a low rumble echoed through the valley.

Suddenly an avalanche was coming right at them!
Tigger bounced everyone to safety in his tree. But
the snow rolled Tigger toward a steep cliff!

199

Doing a perfect Whoop-de-Dooper
Loop-de-Looper Alley-Ooper Bounce,
Roo rescued Tigger.

Taking a long look at little Roo
and his other good friends, Tigger knew
his family had been with him all along.

The next day Tigger gave a party for all his friends.
As a special treat, he gave Roo his heart-shaped locket.
"Now wait half a minute!" Tigger cried excitedly.
"We need to take a family portrait to put in it."
And that's exactly what they did.

WALT DISNEP
PICTURES PRESENTS

DINOSAUR

 RETOLD BY JULIE MICHAELS

The Discovery

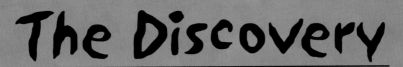

Long, long ago, a lemur named Plio made an exciting discovery. "Dad, get over here!" she cried.

The strange egg she'd found began to crack. Inside was a baby dinosaur!

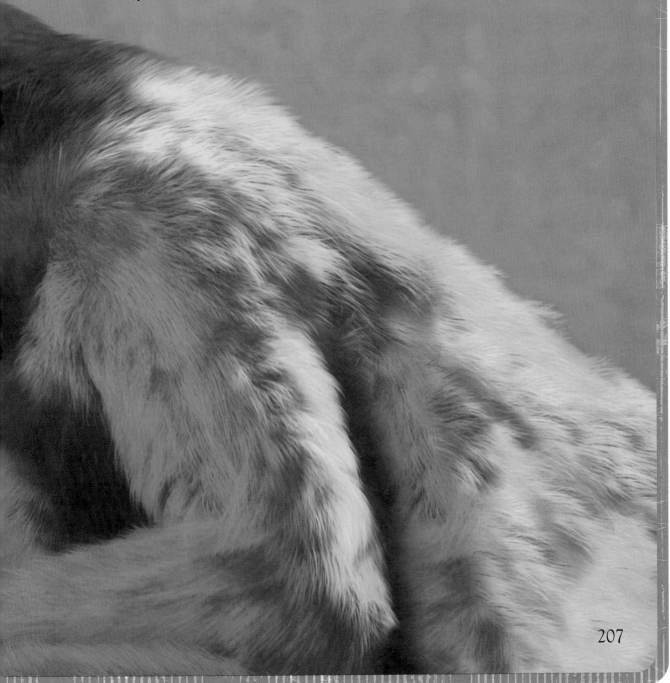

"It's a cold-blooded monster from across the sea," warned Plio's father, Yar.

"It looks like a baby to me," said Plio. And so the dinosaur began his life on Lemur Island.

The lemurs named the dinosaur Aladar, and watched with amazement as the tiny baby grew into a giant iguanodon!

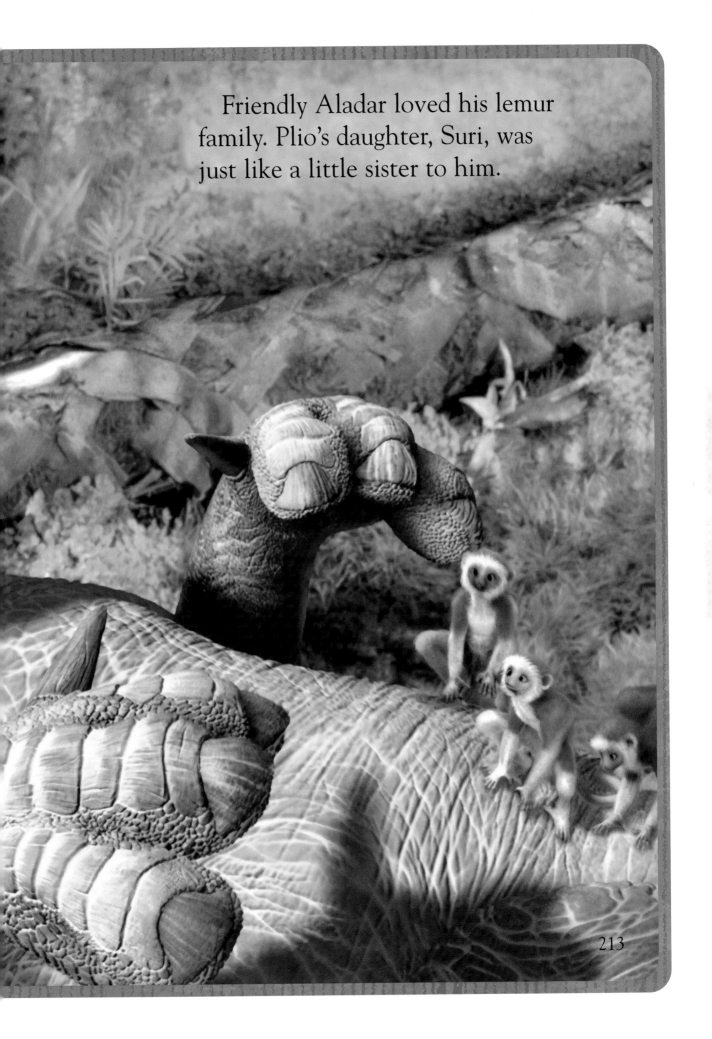

Friendly Aladar loved his lemur
family. Plio's daughter, Suri, was
just like a little sister to him.

One day Plio called the young lemurs: it was time for the courtship ritual.

Lemurs swung through the vines of the Ritual Tree, choosing partners.

But Aladar's friend Zini got hopelessly tangled! "You always have next year," Aladar said kindly.

But Aladar would never find one of his own kind on Lemur Island. "If only there was someone on the island for you," Plio told him.

219

The Fireball

Suddenly a deep stillness fell over the island. "Something's wrong," Yar said grimly. "Aladar, where's Suri?" cried Plio.

Across the sea, a huge meteor had crashed to the earth. Now an enormous wave of fire and water was roaring toward Lemur Island!

Aladar raced across the island, carrying Plio, Suri, Yar, and Zini. Finally he reached a cliff at the edge of the island. With the giant Fireball right behind him, Aladar plunged toward the sea below!

Aladar swam his friends toward the mainland.
Their beautiful island home had been destroyed.

Through a cloud of gathering dust, the small group saw a herd of . . . dinosaurs! "Look at all the Aladars!" cried Suri.

228

Aladar and the lemurs joined the Herd. They met two of the slower dinosaurs, Baylene and Eema.

"The Herd is marching to the Nesting Grounds to have their babies," explained Eema. The trip was difficult: the Fireball had changed much of the land.

Aladar stopped the Herd leader, Kron. "Maybe you could slow it down a bit?" he asked. Baylene and Eema could barely keep up.

"Let the weak set the pace?" Kron thought Aladar was joking.

233

Kron and his scout, Bruton, knew that the Herd needed to find water to survive. And they needed to stay ahead of their enemies, the savage carnotaurs.

234

Aladar struggled to help Eema and Baylene keep pace with the Herd. At last Eema called out, "The lake! It's just over that hill!"

But the Fireball had turned the lake into a dry bed of sunbaked rocks and bones.

Aladar had an idea! If he dug a hole, he might find water beneath the sand.

"Water!" he cried. The Herd stampeded toward the water hole.

Later that night, Aladar noticed Suri trying to coax two small dinosaurs from a cave.

"The little Aladars haven't had anything to drink," she explained.

As Aladar was showing the dinosaurs how to get water, Kron's sister, Neera, approached.

242

Neera thought Aladar was kind to look after the little dinosaurs.

"If we watch out for each other," Aladar explained, "we all stand a better chance of getting to your Nesting Grounds."

Survival

On a nearby hill, a wounded Bruton brought bad news: carnotaurs were coming!

"Move the Herd out—double time!" thundered Kron.

Kron forced Neera along with the Herd. Aladar stayed behind with his slower friends.

As night came on, his little group realized they couldn't find the Herd. But they did find Bruton— the Herd had left him behind, too.

When the rain began, the friends took
refuge in a cave. Even Bruton joined them.
To his surprise, Plio gently nursed his wounds.

Suddenly the carnotaurs entered the cave and attacked Aladar! Bruton pushed into the battle.

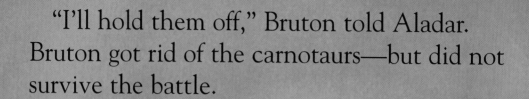

"I'll hold them off," Bruton told Aladar.
Bruton got rid of the carnotaurs—but did not
survive the battle.

253

Aladar and his friends walked deeper into the cave, hoping to find another way out.

Then Zini smelled fresh air! They began digging at the rocks, trying to break through to the outside.

But the digging wasn't working: Aladar
began to give up. "You gave us hope," Baylene
told him. "And I'm going to go on believing it!"
The group gave a big push—they broke through
the wall of rock and into the Nesting Grounds!

The Herd was not in the valley.

Eema looked at a rocky landslide. "That's the way we used to get in," she said worriedly. Aladar knew he had to go back and show the Herd the new way to the Nesting Grounds.

Aladar found Kron urging the Herd over
the dangerous landslide. "There's a safer way!"
he called.

Kron thought Aladar was trying to take
over leadership of the Herd. He knocked
Aladar to the ground.

Neera knocked her brother away from Aladar.
When she and Aladar began walking to the cave, the
Herd followed.

Then a carnotaur appeared! "If we scatter, he'll
pick us off," Aladar told the Herd. "Stand together!"

The carnotaur decided to attack the one dinosaur that stood alone—Kron.

Neera and Aladar ran to help Kron. But they were too late.

Then the carnotaur turned on Neera. But she and Aladar defeated the beast.
Now the Herd could move on.

Some weeks later, Aladar and Neera watched their first baby hatch.

"Oh, oh, happy day!" cheered Eema.

At last the friends had found a new home.

Disney's

1O2
DALMATIANS

 RETOLD BY ZOE BENJAMIN

Cruella on the Loose

Cruella De Vil was free from prison. She was a changed woman. Now she was kind to all animals—even dogs.

The judge warned Cruella that if she ever returned to her puppynapping ways, he would take away her freedom—and her fortune.

274

Cruella's loyal assistant, Alonso, picked her up from prison. He brought her a gift. The frightened, hairless puppy growled at Cruella.

"Look, he's smiling at me," cooed Cruella. She named her new dog Fluffy.

Kevin Shepherd ran the Second Chance Dog Shelter. He loved dogs. He played tug-of-war with Drooler while the other dogs watched.

Waddlesworth, a macaw who thought he was a dog, cheered them on.

But Second Chance was in trouble. Kevin did not have the rent money.

His landlord told him, "You and your mangy pack

are out of here tomorrow!"

"You can't turn all these dogs loose in the city," protested Kevin. But his landlord did not care.

The landlord returned the next day to kick out Kevin and the dogs.

But Cruella had heard about Kevin's misfortune. She decided to buy the shelter!

Chloe Simon was in charge of Cruella's probation. She watched over Cruella to make sure she stayed out of trouble.

"I don't trust anyone who knowingly puts Cruella
De Vil anywhere near dogs!" Chloe told Kevin.

Chloe kept a close eye on Cruella. She saw Cruella transform Second Chance into an animal palace. Cruella even gave the dogs new hairstyles and bubble baths!

Chloe had dogs of her own—Dipstick, Dottie, and their puppies. One day she brought them to work. Agnes, Chloe's boss, met the dogs for the first time. "So you're Domino," she said to the pup with the domino on his collar. "Little Dipper, your tail is just like Daddy's. I know you, Oddball, because you don't have any—"

"Shh!" interrupted Chloe. She knew Oddball felt left out because she hadn't gotten her spots.

Then Cruella came in for her visit. While Chloe was talking to her, the puppies quickly got into trouble. They wound up out on the window ledge! Cruella spotted the endangered pups, and Chloe rescued them.

But something was happening to Cruella. . . .

289

Outside Chloe's open window, Big Ben was chiming loudly. The noise had a strange effect on Cruella. Her hair sprang up wildly. Everywhere she looked she saw spots. She ran from Chloe's office. The cruel was returning to Cruella!

291

Cruel Cruella

Cruella quickly decided that she had to make the Dalmatian puppy coat that she had designed years earlier.

She knew just the furrier to help her—Jean Pierre LePelt. She went to his fur fashion show and enlisted his help.

293

294

Meanwhile, Chloe and Kevin happened to meet up in the park with all their pets. Everyone was enjoying a puppet show when Oddball climbed up on the stage! She wanted to help a spotted puppet.

Oddball ran off the stage and tumbled onto a
balloon seller. Tangled up in balloon strings, Oddball
began floating away!

Kevin begged Waddlesworth to rescue Oddball. But when Waddlesworth hopped from Kevin's hand, he fell to the ground. "Dogs can't fly! Can't fly!" he squawked sadly.

Kevin ran after Oddball and the balloons. He climbed on top of the puppet theater. He jumped for the balloon strings . . . and caught them!

He and Oddball landed safely on a playground slide. Chloe was so happy to have the little pup back.

299

On the other side of town, Cruella and LePelt
worked on a new design for a spotted puppy coat.
Cruella wanted more puppies than ever before.

"We need one hundred and two," she said. "This time I want a *hooded* spotted puppy coat."

Cruella had Alonso steal dozens of Dalmatian puppies. Her assistant was badly bruised and bitten when he returned to her.

She soon had a new mission for him: leave a few of the stolen pups at Second Chance. She wanted to make sure someone else took the blame for her crime.

The next morning, police officers showed up at Kevin's door. They had a phone tip about some stolen Dalmatian pups.

The police found the pups at Second Chance.

"I'm being set up!" protested Kevin. "Why would I steal Dalmatians?"

305

Chloe and Cruella arrived at Second Chance.
"If I'm caught stealing puppies, my fortune goes to
him," Cruella said, pointing at Kevin. "Would that be

a motive?" The police took Kevin and his animals to jail. Chloe was very upset, and Cruella pretended she felt bad, too.

Get Those Puppies!

Cruella invited Chloe and Dipstick to a fancy party at her house. "You need a distraction," she told Chloe.

But the party was just another part of Cruella's heartless plan. She wanted to dognap Chloe's Dalmatian puppies!

As the guests and their dogs ate, Dipstick heard a tiny bark. He saw Fluffy, Cruella's hairless dog, signaling to him. He and Chloe followed Fluffy out of the room.

311

Wanting to help, Fluffy led Dipstick and Chloe to Cruella's fur room. Chloe gasped when she saw the design for the Dalmatian puppy coat!

"Surprise!" cackled Cruella behind them. She locked the door—but not before Dipstick escaped.

313

Dipstick raced home to save his family. Cruella had sent LePelt to dognap the puppies, but they gave him quite a fight. Oddball managed to start the Twilight Bark—soon, dogs all over London were barking the news about the puppynapping.

315

Dipstick arrived home just after LePelt had finally captured Dottie and the puppies. With a giant leap, Dipstick landed in the back of LePelt's truck.

At the jail, Kevin's dogs heard the Twilight Bark. Waddlesworth translated the barks for Kevin. Then Waddlesworth stole the guard's keys and set Kevin and the others free!

317

With Fluffy's help, Chloe escaped from the fur room, and arrived at her apartment at the same time as Kevin.

"Something rotten in Denmark! Rotten in Denmark!" cawed Waddlesworth. Chloe's apartment was ransacked. Her dogs and their dognapper were gone.

Drooler found a train ticket that LePelt had dropped. "The Orient Express at ten!" cried Chloe.

319

Cruella and LePelt were standing outside the train
station examining the puppies LePelt had stolen.
Cruella picked up Oddball. Oddball was wearing a

spotted sweater, but she still did not have any spots of her own. "I asked for spotted dogs!" Cruella shrieked. "And you brought me a white rat!" She dropped Oddball.

The brave pup ran off to find her family.

Oddball found the right train. She raced alongside it as Kevin and Chloe arrived with the others.

Oh no! Oddball was in danger of falling onto the tracks! Waddlesworth flapped into the air, scooped up Oddball, and placed her safely on the train. "Dogs can fly!" he squawked.

Once in Paris, Cruella, Alonso, and LePelt drove to
LePelt's workshop. Alonso put the dogs into the cellar.
Waddlesworth and Oddball had been hiding in

Cruella's car. Now they sneaked into the workshop
and freed the puppies.

When Cruella caught sight of Oddball leading the puppies out of the cellar, she dashed after them. Oddball led the puppies into a bakery next door.

327

The bakery machine started up and . . .
slip–slide–splat! Cruella fell into a vat.
The pups pushed bags of flour into the vat.

Cruella tried, but she couldn't get out of the sticky batter.

Now it was time to bake a cake!

Kevin, Chloe, and Kevin's pets tracked the puppies
to the bakery. When they arrived, they saw that

Cruella was no match for one hundred and two Dalmatians.
The pups had baked her into a Cruella cake!

Kevin and Chloe celebrated with their pets. They found more good news waiting for them in London. The judge was sending Cruella back to prison—and donating her fortune to Second Chance.

And someone else received a special gift, too. There would be no more spotted sweaters for Oddball. She finally had the real thing!

DISNEP'S
THE EMPEROR'S
NEW GROOVE

RETOLD BY NATALYE ABUAN

Spoiled Rotten

Once upon a time, there was a magnificent empire run by Emperor Kuzco. Let's face it: Kuzco was spoiled, rude, and totally obnoxious. And those were his good qualities!

Kuzco had an adviser named Yzma.
She was nasty to all the peasants.
Yzma's assistant was a strong young
man named Kronk. He did things
like swat flies for Yzma—even
if it meant swatting his own
forehead. Duh!

340

Yzma's idea of fun was to sit on Kuzco's throne and pretend to run the empire. This really annoyed Kuzco. So one day he fired her! Yzma was *not* happy about that.

Later that day, a peasant named Pacha was called in to see Kuzco.

Kuzco told Pacha he was going to destroy his village to build a vacation home called Kuzcotopia.

"But where will the people of my village live?" the gentle peasant asked in dismay.

"Hmm," Kuzco said selfishly. "Don't know. Don't care."

What's for Dinner?

Meanwhile, Yzma and Kronk plotted a way to get rid of Kuzco.

"I'll just poison him!" Yzma cried.

That night, Yzma and Kronk held a dinner for Kuzco.

But, as usual, Kronk goofed. He couldn't remember which cup contained the poison.

At last Kuzco drank.

Then something very strange happened. The emperor grew long ears . . . and fur . . . and hooves! He was turning into a llama!

Yzma told Kronk to knock Kuzco out and get rid of him, once and for all.

Kronk had two little advisers. One was an angel and one was a devil.

"You're not just gonna throw him away, are you?" asked the angel.

"Don't listen to that guy!" said the devil.

Kronk was confused. But he still stuffed Kuzco in a sack and headed for the canal.

Then, after dropping the sack containing Kuzco into the canal, Kronk felt terrible. At the last second, he leaped after the sack, and tried to rescue the llama—er—emperor.

But then Kronk tripped. The sack flew out of his hands and onto Pacha's cart! Before Kronk could catch up, Pacha disappeared into the crowd.

Pacha had no idea that the emperor was in a sack on his cart. He was just glad to arrive home to his wife and two children. But he didn't have the heart to tell them the emperor planned to destroy their village.

357

When Pacha opened the strange sack on his cart, a funny-looking llama spoke to him.

"Demon llama!" cried Pacha.

"Oh, wait. I know you!" said Kuzco. "You're that whiny peasant!"

Pacha gasped. "Emperor Kuzco?" he asked in disbelief.

Jungle Bungle

Boy, was Kuzco surprised to find out he was a llama! He demanded that Pacha take him to Yzma. Kuzco thought Yzma would make him human again.

"Not unless you build Kuzcotopia somewhere else," Pacha replied. Kuzco angrily stomped off into the jungle.

"The jungle is dangerous!" warned Pacha.

"La-la-la!" sang Kuzco, ignoring Pacha. "Not listening!"

After tromping through the jungle for a while, Kuzco came upon a cute little squirrel named Bucky. Bucky kindly offered the emperor an acorn. But Kuzco wasn't very grateful.

"Hit the road, Bucky!" he shouted.

Just then, Kuzco tumbled down a hill, waking a pack of jaguars!

364

The jaguars chased him to the edge of a cliff.

Just when it seemed like the end for Kuzco, Pacha swung through the jungle on a vine and rescued him. But then they both fell into a river thousands of feet below!

"You call this a rescue?" Kuzco asked.

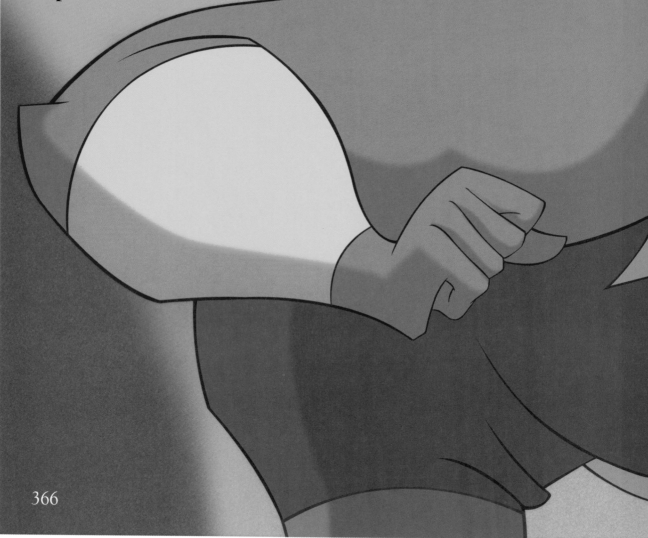

Llama Llama Ding Dong

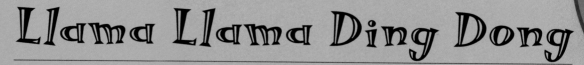

Meanwhile, back at the palace, Yzma was the new ruler.

"Kuzco is dead, right?" she asked.

"Well—he's not as dead as we would have hoped," Kronk replied.

"You bumbling fool!" shrieked Yzma. Yzma ordered Kronk to take her on a search for the missing emperor–llama.

Night fell in the jungle. Pacha draped his poncho over Kuzco as he went to sleep.

The next morning, Kuzco said something he had never said before in his life: "Uh, thanks."

He also agreed not to destroy Pacha's village to build Kuzcotopia.

Pacha was thrilled!

369

Of course, Kuzco was lying. He didn't think he
needed Pacha anymore. He laughed as Pacha fell
through a broken bridge!

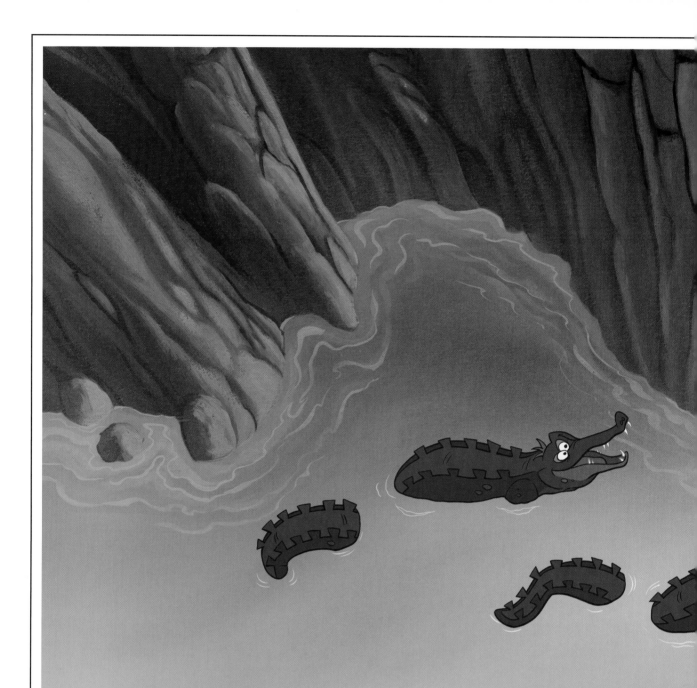

But then Kuzco fell, too! Now they both had to climb back up.

Pacha realized that they would have to work together. Carefully, the two made their way up the cliff.

At the top of the cliff, a piece of rock crumbled under Pacha's feet! Luckily, Kuzco reached out and saved him.

"I knew there was some good in you!" Pacha said.

Meanwhile, Yzma and Kronk met Bucky the squirrel, who told them all about a talking llama.

They knew the llama must be Kuzco.

375

Kuzco's Shocking Discovery

Pacha took Kuzco, disguised as his bride, to a funky jungle restaurant called Mudka's Meat Hut. "Heeheehee," giggled Pacha as he gave the waitress their order. "We're on our honeymoon!"

Pacha overheard Yzma and Kronk in the restaurant plotting against Kuzco.

"They're trying to kill you!" Pacha warned Kuzco.
Kuzco didn't believe Pacha until he overheard them himself.

"If you hadn't mixed up those potions," Yzma said to Kronk, "Kuzco would be dead!"
Kuzco was stunned. They *had* tried to kill him.

378

Alone and frightened, Kuzco ran to find Pacha. But Pacha was gone. For the first time, Kuzco realized how important it was to have a friend.

Later, in the jungle, Kronk awoke from a deep sleep. He remembered that the man in the restaurant—Pacha—was the same peasant he had seen leaving the city with Kuzco on his cart. If they found Pacha, they would find Kuzco!

Kronk, for once, was right: Kuzco *was* with
Pacha. Kuzco had found his one true friend
among a herd of llamas.

But Kuzco wasn't out of trouble yet! Yzma and Kronk were headed right toward Pacha's house to find Pacha and Kuzco. Luckily, Pacha got his family to stall the evil pair while Pacha and Kuzco headed off to the palace!

Race to the Palace!

It didn't take Yzma long to figure out she had been tricked. She and Kronk caught up with Pacha and Kuzco and chased them through the jungle. When they came to a cliff, Pacha and Kuzco swung to the other side. Kronk and Yzma tried to follow them across, but they were hit by a bolt of lightning. Yikes!

When they finally got to the palace, Kuzco and Pacha raced to the lab. But while they were searching for the potion that would change Kuzco back into a human, Yzma suddenly appeared. "Finish them off!" she told Kronk.

Once again, Kronk was confused. It didn't seem right to get rid of Pacha and Kuzco. So Yzma dropped him through a trapdoor.

389

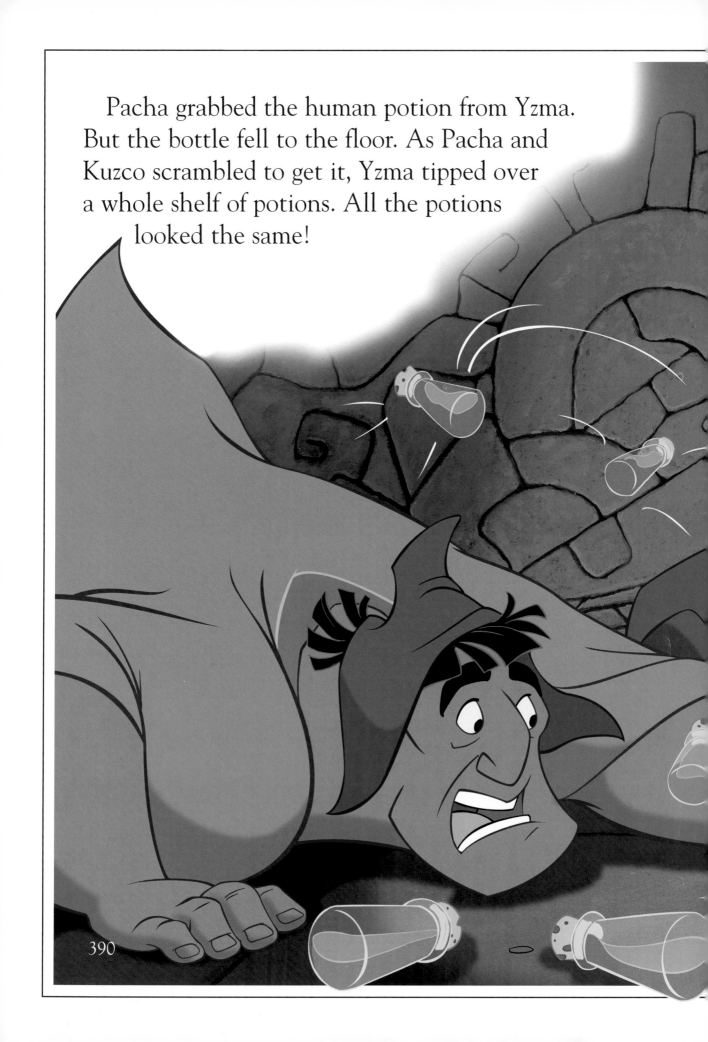

Pacha grabbed the human potion from Yzma.
But the bottle fell to the floor. As Pacha and
Kuzco scrambled to get it, Yzma tipped over
a whole shelf of potions. All the potions
looked the same!

390

Kuzco to the Rescue

Yzma called the guards, who chased Kuzco and Pacha outside the palace. Kuzco and Pacha had just two bottles left! One would make Kuzco human again. But Yzma got ahold of one of the bottles. It turned her into a cat!

Now they were down to the last bottle! Kuzco knew it must be the one that would make him human again.

Suddenly Pacha slipped. He grabbed onto the palace wall, but was losing his grip. Kuzco had to choose: either take the potion, or save Pacha's life.

Finally, Kuzco actually did the right thing: he saved Pacha. But Yzma had the human potion!

Just then Kronk opened the door, and accidentally flattened Yzma the kitty!

She dropped the potion, and Pacha caught it. Kuzco could finally become human again.

396

Later, Kuzco decided to build his summer home on a different hill.

Pacha smiled. He knew that Kuzco was sparing his village but was too embarrassed to admit he was doing something nice.

Kronk turned out to be a great camp counselor for all the kids in Pacha's village. With Bucky's help, he even taught them how to speak squirrel.

Soon, Kuzco was enjoying village life in a small hut, built on the hill right next to Pacha's.

It wasn't Kuzcotopia, but Kuzco was happy anyway. For the first time in his life, he felt loved and at home.